MOLEHOLE MYSTERIES

SECRET AT
MOSSY ROOTS
MANSION

DATE DUE		
JUL 13		
APR 2 2		
MAY 0 9		
SEP 5		
MAR 0 5 1998		

Written by
Barbara Davoll

Pictures by Dennis Hockerman

MOODY PRESS

Moody Press, a ministry of the Moody Bible Institute,
is designed for education, evangelization, and edifi-
cation. If we may assist you in knowing more about
Christ and the Christian life, please write us without
obligation: Moody Press, c/o MLM, Chicago, IL 60610.
Printed in MEXICO.

ISBN: 0-8024-2701-4

Children love the stories of Barbara Davoll, known for her award-winning, best-selling Christopher Churchmouse Classics and now for the Molehole Mystery series. Barbara writes these zany new adventures in Schroon Lake, New York where she and her husband, Roy, minister at home and abroad with Word of Life International in their Missions Department. Barb manages to stay busy as a wife, mother, grandmother, author, drama teacher, church musician, and homemaker for her husband and Josh, the family Schnauzer.

Illustrator Dennis Hockerman has concentrated on art for children's trade books and textbooks, magazines, greeting cards, and games. He lives with his wife and three children in Mequon, Wisconsin, a suburb of Milwaukee. Mr. Hockerman probably spent more time "underground" than above while developing the characters and creating the etchings for the Molehole Mysteries. Periodically, he would poke his head into his "upstairs connection" to join his family and share with them the adventures of his friends in Molesbury R.F.D.

Contents

1

THE FRIGHT

Just outside the village of Molesbury R. F. D., on the way to the town of Diggerton, is a hidden path. This path winds back from the road to a small shack tucked among roots and brambles. A crooked sign, hanging above the door of the shack, gives a clue. It says,

MOLEHOLE MYSTERY CLUB

DUSTY AND MUSTY MOLE, JUNIOR AGENTS

Scrawled underneath these words is a warning:

KEEP OUT! MEMBERS ONLY! THIS MEANS YOU!

On this warm summer afternoon a hum of mole voices could be heard through the boarded up window. The Molehole Mystery Club was in session.

"We'll never get to the bottom of this if we don't find some more clues," growled Snarkey Mole. "How can Muston Mole be mixed up in this if he weren't in town?"

"We don't know for sure he was out of town when Moriah's medal was stolen," argued Mortimer Mole. 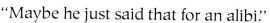 "Maybe he just said that for an alibi."

"What's an alibi?" asked Penelope. Her narrow mole eyes opened wide.

"Aw, for Pete's sake, Penelope, I don't know how you ever passed the test to get in this club," snorted Alfred Mole in disgust. "Don't you know anything about detective work? An alibi is a made-up excuse. You should know that *if* you know anything at all about solving crimes."

"Hold it, Alfred. There's no need to be nasty," soothed Dusty Mole, the junior agent. "Penney is new here, and we need to help her learn the terms."

"Maybe I could go down to Muston's tonight and see if I can pick up any clues," suggested Otis Mole.

He was a chubby little mole, who was a charter member of the club.

"Naw, you can't do it, Otis. You're too—well, you're too much of a chub," said Alfred. "You'd never squeeze into Muston's small hole. I probably should do it," he continued proudly, smoothing the fur on his sleek body. "I'm well built and I—"

"Well, I say we give up on this one," interrupted Snarkey. "We've been working on this case for weeks.

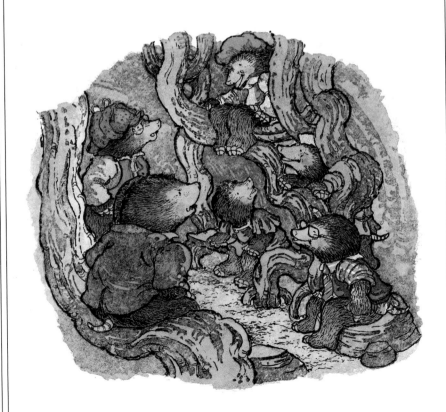

Frankly I'm getting fed up with it. We need a new case. The reason we can't find any clues is because old Moriah just made up the story to get attention."

Snarkey had spent some time working with the famous Squirrelock Holmes as an undercover agent.* He was older and more experienced than the other moles in the club. "Squirrelock would never waste his time on such a case," he snorted. "There's not a doubt in my mind. Old Moriah made it all up."

"Snarkey! What a terrible thing to say about poor Mr. Moriah," cried Penelope in a shocked voice. "Why, he would never do that! I'm ashamed of you!" she sputtered, wagging her claw at him.

"Come on, you guys! Cut it out!" shouted Dusty. "We're just getting all riled up at each other."

Just then there was the sound of running feet on the path outside.

"Guard the door," yelled Mortimer. "Don't let anyone in without the password!"

At that moment someone barged into the clubhouse. "What's the password?" growled Mortimer, barring the door with his body.

"Cluehouse," gasped a mole, panting for breath.

"Musty! What do you mean flying in here like that and scaring us to death!" fumed Mortimer. "What's the big idea?"

"Oh, close the door, Morty!" cried Musty, looking behind her fearfully. "It may be after me!" She ran to hide behind her twin brother, Dusty.

"Settle down, Musty. There's nothing out there," he soothed, looking out through a crack in the wall.

"Oh yes there is!" insisted Musty. The little girl mole was nearly hysterical with fright.

"What did you see, Sis?" asked Dusty. He knew his sister would never cry in front of all the club members if she weren't really upset.

"Come on now. This isn't like Musty Mole, Junior Agent," he jibed. "You act like you've seen a ghost."

Musty, who was trying to stop crying, looked up. Her eyes were wide and fearful, and she was shaking all over.

"Th—that's just what I s—saw," she stuttered. "I saw a g—ghost!" She started to cry again.

THE MEDAL

"Ha! Just like a girl," snorted Mortimer. "I told you girls shouldn't be allowed in the club. They're just a bunch of sissies!" Mortimer was prejudiced against girls. His prejudice showed itself in various ways, often in angry words.

"I am not a sissy, Mortimer Mole!" sobbed Musty, stamping her foot. "You take that back right now!"

In the past Dusty had felt the same way as Mortimer about girls. But when Musty helped solve the mystery involving Sammy Shrew's drug ring, he had changed his mind. Then he asked her to be his partner and a junior agent. He had a new respect for her now.

"Where did you see this *alleged* ghost?" he asked in his most serious junior agent voice.

Taking a big breath to calm herself, Musty began. "I had been down to Muston Mole's house, searching his yard for clues, when I realized I was late for Club. I left Muston's and thought I would take a shortcut through Mossy Roots Swamp."

"Oh," gasped Penelope, with her paw over her mouth. "That's a terrible place! Why did you ever go through there?"

"Because I was late, Penney. I didn't want to pay the late fee that Mortimer *insists* we must pay," she retorted, giving a hard look at Morty, who was slouched in a corner listening.

"Go on, Musty," said Otis, looking tenderly at her. He had a big crush on the cute little girl mole.

*This story is found in Molehole Mystery Book 1, *Dusty Mole, Private Eye*.

"Well, I didn't think it would be so bad to take the shortcut during the day," reasoned Musty. "But once I was in the swamp, I was sorry. It was s—so dark and s—scary alone."

Dusty gulped. He probably would have thought twice himself before going through the swamp. His sister was braver than he thought.

"I was climbing over some thick brambles and got my skirt caught on a thorn," said Musty. "As I was trying to get loose, I heard a noise. Just a few feet away from me was a big old house, hidden in the roots of a huge tree. It was an old mansion, all overgrown with moss and brambles. I thought it looked like a—a haunted house."

"Probably the old Madagascar Mansion," said Alfred, who was a quiet scholarly type. "The Town Hall shows a deed for a piece of property in the swamp in his name."

"The house was spooky looking, with the windows boarded up and the porch falling off," went on Musty. "But it was the noise that bothered me. There was an eerie sound coming from the house. While I was trying to get loose, I realized what the sound was."

"What was it?" asked Penelope fearfully, holding her breath.

"It was like someone wailing or crying. I mean—like they were dying or something. It was then—I s—saw it. I saw something white in the darkness. It came out of the door of the house and into the swamp. It was coming right toward me!"

"Oohh!" gasped Penelope. "I'd have been scared spitless!"

"I couldn't get loose because of the brambles, so I ducked down behind some roots and hid. The white thing was still coming toward me. I could hear it wailing as it came through the brambles. It—it was *real*, I tell you. It was a ghost! A real—*ghost* mole!"

Dusty stood with his paw around her, looking at first one and then another of the club members. They were staring in disbelief. *The ghost could not make noise if it were not real.*

"Aw, what would you expect from a girl?" jibed Mortimer. "She just got upset and *thought* she saw something."

"Then how do you explain this, Morty?" asked Musty, calmer now. She held out something shiny.

"The medal! You've found Moriah's gold medal!" shrieked Penelope.

All the moles crowded around to see the object in Musty's hand.

"Yes, I did. The ghost dropped it as it went by," said Musty, with a strange look on her face. "It dropped it right in front of the brambles where I was hiding. It never even knew I was there."

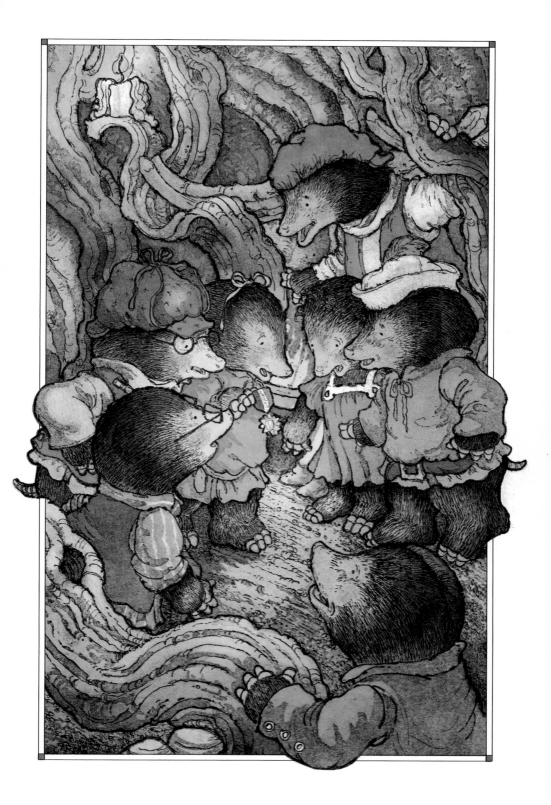

The stunned moles stared in shocked silence. Musty had just recovered the missing medal. Could it be they hadn't found any clues because it had been stolen by a *ghost?*

THE PASSWORD

The members of the Molehole Mystery Club stared at the gold medal in Musty's hand. For weeks they had searched for clues, only to find nothing. Now Musty had found it. It was hard to believe.

Snarkey Mole was the first to speak. "Good grief, Musty! You mean he just dropped it in front of you?"

"He?" asked Musty. "Who says it was a he? I *told you* it was a *ghost*. I couldn't tell if it was a he or she."

"Well, it wasn't a girl, that's for sure," replied Mortimer. "No *girl* would be brave enough to be out in Mossy Roots Swamp."

"My sister was," retorted Dusty quietly. "I don't appreciate all your remarks, Morty. Musty and Penelope are part of this club, and if you don't like it, you can quit."

Mortimer looked at Dusty. He knew he meant business. "Sure, Dusty. I know they are. I just meant that I don't think any girl mole would be living out there in some old run-down mansion."

"Morty's right," agreed Snarkey. "It's got to be a boy. I still don't think it was a ghost though. You probably saw some white piece of cloth or—or something."

"But Musty said the ghost made noise when it walked," reasoned Alfred. He was the most level-headed of the club members. Usually he could find and explain many clues the others missed.

"Well, I think it's wonderful that Musty found the medal," said her supporter Otis. "Now we can close this case and get on to another."

"Not so fast, Pudge," replied Snarkey. "We still don't know who took the medal and why."

"Snark is right," agreed Dusty. "Just because we have the medal proves nothing. We still have a job to do."

"It appears some of us need to go to the scene of the crime," said Alfred practically.

"You—you mean Mossy Roots Swamp?" asked Penelope fearfully.

Alfred nodded his head, as did Dusty.

Penelope looked at Musty with fear and said, "Th—that's a great idea, Alfie, but my mother told me to come home early."

"It's OK, Penney," interrupted Musty. "We're not
fraidies! If anybody is going into the swamp, we'll go
with them and show the way. I'm sure my best friend
will come along. Right, Penney?"

"S—sure, Musty," gulped Penney. Penney's heart was
in her throat as she thought about the dark swamp and
going there. But she couldn't stay in the Club if she
weren't brave. Musty was her good friend, and she
didn't want to be left behind.

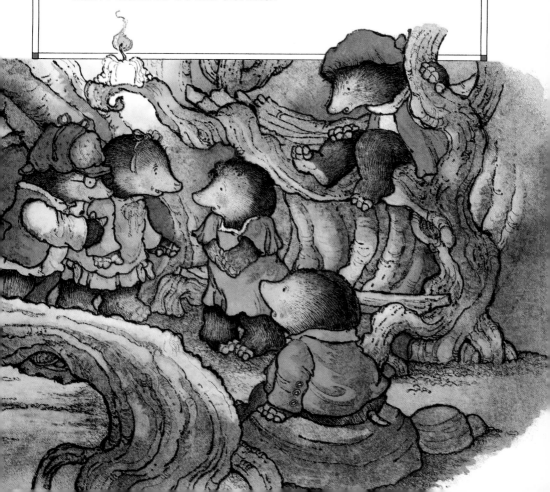

"Well, let's get going!" said Snarkey with excitement. "Give us our assignments, Dusty."

Dusty had been writing something in his notebook. Now he looked up and said, "I'd like you and Alfred to go to Moriah Mole's house. Tell him we have his medal. Try to find out if he was anywhere near the swamp when he lost it."

Snarkey looked at Dusty. "Not on your life," he responded. "I'm not wasting my time going to that old mole's house. I can get some fresh leads in Mossy Roots Swamp. Let the girls take the easy jobs."

"This is no easy job, Snark. Why do you think I'm sending Alfie with you? I need someone with experience to figure out how this alleged ghost took the medal. Take it or leave it," Dusty insisted firmly.

"OK. We'll do it. But the next time I'm doing something with a challenge," agreed Snarkey.

When Dusty had recruited his friends to be in the club, they had all agreed to have him be the leader, with Musty as his partner. This always rubbed some fur the wrong way.

"Otis, I want you to stand guard at the entrance to the swamp. Stay out of sight, and give your whistle if you see any danger."

Otis nodded. He respected Dusty highly and always did whatever he was asked, unless he got stuck somewhere and couldn't get out.

Looking at his notebook again, Dusty continued the assignments. "Morty, I want you to go with me and the girls. We'll approach the mansion from the rear and see what we can find. Remember 'Cluehouse'!" he said, putting out his right paw.

The other moles gathered in a circle, putting their right paws on top of Dusty's. "Cluehouse," they chorused. This password and pledge meant they would put each other's safety first when on a dangerous assignment. They must not run away but help where needed. It was a good rule and often necessary. All knew it would be needed this time.

THE SWAMP

Otis, Mortimer, Dusty, and the girl moles started off,
using the shortcut Musty had taken from the swamp.
All felt they were on the way to high adventure. Musty's
heart was pounding with fear and excitement.

What if we don't see the ghost? she thought. *They'll
think I just made it all up.* No matter what happened,
she knew what she had seen. *Will I see it again?* she
wondered. She half feared she would, and then she
feared she wouldn't.

Dusty and his friends walked along briskly, enjoying the late afternoon warmth. The Underground smelled of growing things in the summer.

"Look!" cried Penelope. "The carrots are getting fatter."

Dusty laughed. "So are our rabbit friends." He pointed to a carrot patch that was being raided by Bulge Bunny. "The people Upstairs had better pull these carrots now if they want any to eat. The rabbits will have them eaten soon."

As the moles approached the swamp, Musty glanced around nervously. There was a tight knot of fear in her tummy. She dreaded going into that dark tangled mess again.

"Here we are," whispered Dusty. "Otis, that thorn bush over there looks like a good place for you to hide and keep guard. We shouldn't be long. Give us an hour. Then wait fifteen more minutes. If you hear nothing from us by then, go get Alf and Snark and come in after us."

"Got it," said Otis. "I'll whistle if I see anything out here." The chunky little mole began to make his way through the brambles and thorns to his hiding place.

"We should move slowly," said Mort. "We don't want to make a lot of noise and scare the ghost away."

"That's right," agreed Dusty. "I'll go first with Musty. You two follow. Let's go."

The moles entered the swamp, picking their way carefully over dead roots, brambles, and painful thorns. It was tough going. The thorns grabbed their fur and slowed their progress. Their feet got wet from the swampy soil.

Inside the swamp it was pitch black. Although the moles were used to the darkness of the underground, this was different. As they grew accustomed to the blackness, they could see a bit better.

"Do you know where the mansion is?" Morty asked Musty.

"I'm pretty sure," she said. "I think it's just over to the left of that clump of roots."

The moles plodded through the swamp the way Musty suggested.

"It's not here," said the little girl mole with dis-appointment. "I'm sure it was—no, wait a minute. It might have been to the right of the clump of roots."

"Let's go back then," said Dusty, leading the way.

The moles made their way back to the clump of roots and headed to the right.

"It isn't here either," cried Musty. "It's so confusing," she complained. "Everything looks the same. Maybe it's straight ahead."

"Grab paws, guys," said Dusty, as he started plowing through the muck. "We don't want to get separated in here."

The girl moles eagerly grabbed paws, but Morty said, "Aw, I don't need to hang onto any girl. I'm all right."

"Mortimer, do as I say," whispered Dusty.

There was no answer. "Mort? Did you hear what I said? We need to hang onto each other and not get separated. Are you hearing me, Mortimer?"

"He—he isn't back here, Dusty," whispered Penelope in a strangled tone.

"What! He just was. What do you mean?" The boy mole came to an abrupt halt.

"I—I don't know. He just disappeared!"

"He's probably caught in some thorns. I'll find him. You girls stay put. I'll go get him." With that Dusty started off through the swamp, calling Mort's name in a loud whisper.

The girl moles waited for what seemed hours for Dusty to return. Actually it was only a few minutes. They were relieved when they heard him coming.

"I can't find him," Dusty said with concern.

"Wh—what's happened to him, Dusty?" asked his sister. "He was right here with us."

"I know. I've heard there's quicksand in here. I'm wondering—"

"Oh no! You don't think he could have fallen into quicksand, do you?" cried Penney.

5

THE GHOST

"How will we ever find Mortimer in here?" cried Dusty's twin. "It's terrible to think he may be struggling in quicksand."

"I think we'd have heard him yell, if that happened," reasoned the leader. *Maybe he slipped away to do some sleuthing on his own,* he thought. He had not wanted to hold onto the girls.

If Mort was in danger, Dusty must do something quickly to rescue him. If the headstrong mole had gone off on his own, he could get into big trouble. They couldn't look for the ghost until they found him.

"Dusty!" cried Musty. "I know the way now! I remember that knot of thorns. That's where I was caught. The mansion has to be right over there."

Quickly Dusty made the decision to head in the direction she was pointing. Mortimer was not to be found here. "Let's go," he whispered, holding onto his sister tightly.

Slowly the moles moved the way Musty had shown. And just then they heard it! All three moles froze. A low moan came from just ahead.

Shivers of fear washed over the little animals. "Move slowly!" warned Dusty. Silently they inched forward.

"EEEOOOEE!" A scream from Penelope pierced the air! There was a sound of struggle from behind, and then a guttural voice said, "Don't move, or you're history."

Dusty whirled around. In doing so, he caught himself on a thorn.

"Musty, I'm caught! Help me here."

While Musty struggled to free Dusty, the sound of the struggle with Penney continued.

Finally Dusty was free and came up behind Penney's captor. Wrapping his paws around the animal that held her, he yelled for Penney to run. As Dusty held the animal, Penney jumped free.

"I give up," cried the animal. The voice sounded strangely familiar.

"Musty, help me hold him," cried her twin. Turning the animal around he said, "Mortimer! It's you! Where have you been?"

"You scared us to death, Mort!" cried Musty, who was holding the shaken Penney and trying to comfort her.

"I told you to stay with us, Mortimer. What do you mean by going off by yourself?" demanded Dusty.

"I'm sorry," apologized Morty. "I couldn't see in the dark, and I thought Penney was the ghost. Musty didn't seem to know where she was going. I thought I could find the mansion faster by myself."

Just then there was a creaking sound and another low wail. "What—what should we do, Dusty?" asked Mortimer.

"We need to get closer. Let's circle around behind the mansion."

"No, Dusty," whispered Musty, pointing ahead. "There's no need. The ghost is coming out the front door."

Hiding in the thorns, the fascinated moles watched as the creaky door opened. A white figure moved off the rickety porch and toward them. Right in front of their eyes was Musty's ghost!

The moles scarcely breathed. Penelope thought her heart would explode with fear. As the white figure moved, they could hear the sounds he made breaking through the roots and thorns. *One thing about this ghost,* thought Dusty. *He doesn't float.*

The ghost lumbered in front of them, giving a low sigh as he passed. Musty's paw was on Dusty's, and she whispered, "Doesn't he sound sad?"

"I guess you'd be sad too if you were dead," her brother responded.

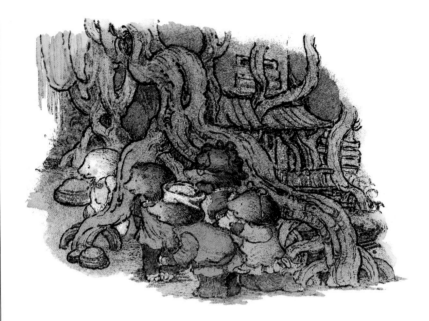

"Oohh, do you really think he is?" asked Musty.

"He sure makes a lot of noise for something dead," observed Mortimer. "Should we follow him?"

They could still see the white animal moving slowly away into the swamp.

"Not now," replied Dusty. "It will take us some time to get back, and our time is nearly up. Otis will be ready for Plan B if we don't get back."

Just then a whistle split the air.

"Otis!" said Dusty. "That's the danger signal! Let's get out of here!"

The moles began fighting their way back through the swamp.

"Do you know which way we came?" asked Mortimer, breathlessly.

"I think so. Put the girls between us and grab paws. Don't let go for anything."

Suddenly, Penelope screamed, "Morty! What's happening!" Mort's big paw had slipped away from hers. "Stop!" she screamed. "Mort's in trouble!"

"Help," cried Morty in a far-away voice. Just seconds before he had been holding onto Penney. Now she could barely see and hear him.

"Dusty!" he screamed desperately. "It's quicksand! I'm sinking! Help!"

They heard another of Otis's danger whistles. Frantically the moles scrambled to where Mortimer was slowly sinking out of sight.

THE SHREW

When the frightened moles made their way back to Mortimer trapped in the quicksand, he was a pathetic sight. Only his head was above the black gook.

"Can you get your paws free, Mort?" yelled Dusty.

"I'm trying," shouted the trapped mole. With a struggle Morty was able to free one paw.

"Girls, form a chain and hold onto me," shouted Dusty. "I'm going to lean over the quicksand and grab him."

The girls linked paws and formed a chain, holding onto Dusty. They knew his life and Mort's depended on them.

At first Dusty couldn't reach Mort, but by leaning farther he touched him. Stretching farther still, he locked his paw with Mort's large one.

It was a desperate struggle for life. Mort was gradually being pulled free. If they could only hold on long enough! Each of the moles was stretched to the limit. Their muscles screamed in pain.

In one final heave Morty came flying out of the horrible pit. He looked like some huge black monster, dripping black muck.

Mortimer fell down beside the quicksand pit, trying to get his breath. Penelope was beside him on her knees, wiping the black stuff from his face, mouth, and eyes.

"Thanks, guys!" said Morty, when he could finally speak. "I was a goner if you hadn't come!"

Just then Otis whistled the danger signal again.

"Oh, we've got to get out of here," whispered Musty in alarm. "Why do you suppose he's whistling?"

"I don't know, but we need to scram," said Dusty. "Musty, you'll have to lead the way. I'll help Mort. Let's go!"

With great difficulty the moles made their way through the swamp. Dusty held onto Morty, who lumbered along awkwardly, exhausted from his struggle. Another whistle signal guided them to the entrance of the swamp.

Otis watched horrified as they emerged. He could hardly believe his eyes as he stared at black, dripping Mortimer.

"What happened?" Otis asked, running to meet them.

"Morty fell in the quicksand, and we had to rescue him," explained Musty. "That happened just as we heard your first signal."

"What's up, Otis?" demanded Dusty. "Why did you signal us?"

Looking around as though he feared someone would hear, Otis said softly, "You had company."

"What do you mean?" questioned the leader.

"Sammy Shrew and a couple of his thugs went into the swamp when I whistled. They're in there now!"

"Sammy Shrew!" Musty cried. Penelope clutched at Musty in fear.

"Is he the horrible shrew who tried to sell you drugs?" Penney quavered.

"He's the one," grunted Dusty. "Are you sure, Otis? I thought they had him behind bars for life."

"They did," answered his friend. "I overheard them talking about his escape from jail. They were talking about the swamp mansion. Sounds as though they'd like to use it as a hideout."

"Well, they'll have a surprise waiting for them there," said Mortimer.

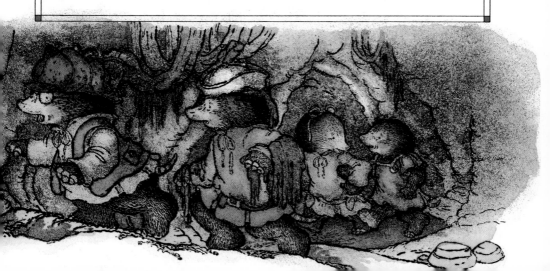

"Did you see the ghost?" asked Otis eagerly.

"Yes, we did," answered Dusty. "And I don't think he's a ghost. There's something funny going on. This ghost is very much alive."

All the moles stared at their leader. *What would happen to the ghost if Sammy Shrew found it before they did?*

7

THE ENCOUNTER

The next day Dusty was up early. He knew they must move quickly now that Sammy Shrew and his thugs were loose in the swamp. Somehow Dusty felt sorry for the swamp ghost. He smiled to himself, thinking he was actually beginning to like a ghost.

The junior agent put on his Squirrelock Holmes hat and picked up his magnifying glass and fingerprint kit. Then he quietly left his molehole.

The early morning fog rolled through the underground, giving an eerie look to familiar objects. Dusty made his way quietly along the tunnels that led to Mossy Root Swamp.

Having reached the swamp, Dusty plowed through the muck to the thornbush where Musty had been caught. He couldn't see the swamp mansion in the fog, but he knew it was there. All seemed quiet. *I wonder if Sammy and his thugs are in there?* he wondered.

Dusty settled down to wait, well-hidden in the thorns. Soon he was rewarded. Coming out of the house were Sammy and two of his men. Dusty strained to hear their conversation.

"That was the worst night's sleep I've ever had," growled a thug. "I hardly closed my eyes all night."

"Me either," grunted another. "I kept hearing weird noises all night long. Sounded like someone crying."

"You two are wimps," snarled Sammy Shrew. "You heard the wind howling. Nothing more."

"I sure hope so, Sammy. It might have been someone nosing around like that silly Dusty Mole. He could turn us in to the police."

"That fool?" snapped Sammy. "Never! Not again. He won't find us back here in the swamp. Now let's get out of here and get on with our business."

Dusty smiled as the thugs passed by his hiding place. *Fool, am I?* he thought. *We'll see.*

Dusty moved closer to the old mansion. It did have a haunted-house look, as Musty had said. Silently he moved up onto the rickety porch, picking his way carefully over the rotten floorboards. Standing on tiptoe he peered into the window of the door. It was then that he heard the crying sound again.

The crying became louder as he waited. Through the window he saw movement. A white figure moved into the hall and stood with its back to the window. It was slouched over with its head in its hands. The sound of its crying was so pathetic that Dusty could hardly stand it.

Dusty stood with his mouth open, gaping at the ghost. *It's a mole!* he thought with excitement. *A completely white ghost mole!* The ghost continued to cry as Dusty watched. Finally the junior agent felt he had to make a move. *How do you help a ghost?* wondered the mole detective.

Tapping on the window, Dusty waved to the ghost. It jumped to the side of the door and peeked around at Dusty. Dusty smiled and waved. The ghost drew back and then stuck its head around again, looking at him.

"May I come in?" yelled Dusty through the window. "I won't hurt you. I want to be your friend."

The ghost stared.

Again the detective mole shouted through the window. "Please open the door. I want to help you. Don't be afraid of me."

Slowly the ghost came out where Dusty could see him. Dusty's heart was pounding in his chest. *Will the ghost let me in?* he wondered.

8

THE ALBINO

As Dusty watched, the handle of the front door began to turn slowly. Then the door opened just a crack. Dusty moved quietly over in front of the door and said again, "Please let me come in. I want to be your friend." The door opened a bit wider.

"My name is Dusty Mole. I would love to talk with you."

The door opened a bit more, and a white mole face appeared in the crack. "Are you sure you want to come in?" asked the other mole.

"Oh yes, I really do!" said Dusty with enthusiasm. "I would like to be your friend."

"Well, all right," agreed the mole in the mansion. "Just for a little while." The door opened revealing a small white mole. The most surprising thing about the white mole were his eyes. They were very narrow slits, just like Dusty's, but they were pink! *Maybe this mole is a girl*, thought the junior agent, who was always looking for clues.

Aloud he said, "Hello. I'm Dusty, and I'm pleased to meet you!" As he spoke, Dusty entered the dreary hallway of the old mansion.

"Pleased to meet you," said the ghost mole shyly, tucking his head down as though embarrassed.

"What's your name?" asked Dusty kindly.

"I don't have one," mumbled the white mole. He seemed to ignore the paw Dusty had extended to him.

"You don't have—a name?" questioned Dusty in a surprised tone.

The colorless mole shook his head. "My parents didn't give me one," he said sadly. A silent tear slipped down his white face.

"Oh, I am sorry," responded Dusty kindly. The junior agent slipped his paw around the other mole's shoulders. "It really doesn't matter. I'll just call you Friend," he finished brightly.

"Thank you," said the shy mole quietly. "Would you— would you like to sit down?" he asked, pointing toward the living room.

"Oh yes, very much," answered Dusty. They walked into the room where Dusty had seen the mole crying.

The white mole sat down on an old sofa, and Dusty sat beside him. *I might as well ask,* he thought.

"Are you—well—are you a ghost?" he blurted out.

The white animal looked at him sadly. Dusty saw his narrow pink eyes fill with tears. They began to run down his face like tiny rivers. Dusty watched, fascinated. He thought perhaps they would wash off the white and then the mole would be a normal, brown color. There was no change, however.

"I'm sorry to upset you so," said the brown mole. "I just wanted to know if you're a ghost. It doesn't make any difference—"

"It's all right," interrupted the different mole with a sigh. "Everyone thinks so. But I'm not." The tears continued falling into little puddles on the white mole's fur.

"You're not! Why—that's wonderful!" exploded Dusty with relief. "I mean, you see, we were sort of scared."

"I know," sighed the mole. "Everyone is. I guess that's why I don't have any—friends." A fresh batch of tears filled the lonely mole's eyes. "That's why I have to live in this awful place."

Dusty felt like crying himself. He put his paw around the little mole and patted him awkwardly. "Oh, but I'm sure if animals would just get to know you, they would like you. Why, I like you very much."

"You do?" responded the other mole in astonishment. "But you don't know."

"Know what?" questioned Dusty.

"Why I'm different," whispered the white mole, looking around as though someone might be listening.

"Why are you—different?" questioned Dusty in a kind way.

"I'm an—albino mole," he whispered solemnly.

Dusty sat in stunned silence as the white mole made his confession. *An albino mole?* thought the junior agent. *What on earth is that?*

Instead of voicing his thoughts he said, "Is that so bad?"

"Oh yes!" responded the white animal. "Animals think I'm a ghost or that there is something terribly wrong with me. They are so prejudiced against me I can't even go to school. Even my own parents have rejected me." And the little white mole began to sob as though his heart would break.

"Why would your parents do that?" questioned Dusty.

"Well," said the mole, trying to stop crying, "they were just like everyone else. They were embarrassed. They didn't understand about being an albino."

Neither do I, thought Dusty. *But I must help this poor animal.*

THE PREJUDICE

"I want to help you if I can," said Dusty. "Please tell me more."

The mole went on. "My parents didn't understand that an albino animal is one that doesn't have the right skin and fur pigments. That's what makes my fur white."

At last we're getting to the bottom of this mystery, thought Dusty. With excitement he said, "Is that all?"

"Just that and my—pink eyes," said the mole with disgust. "Most guys think I look like a girl because they're pink. They won't have anything to do with me."

Dusty knew that was what he had thought too. He felt bad, but how could he have known? He had never seen or heard of an albino animal before. He was so relieved to know there was nothing really wrong with his new friend. It was just that he was made differently.

"My parents didn't want me because they didn't understand. I was left alone in the woods during a snowstorm and almost froze to death. I came to this old house during that storm as a baby mole, and I've been here ever since. I can never go outside the swamp. It's too dangerous," he finished sadly.

"That's terrible!" exploded Dusty. "Something has to be done about this. You mean, you've never been to school?"

The sad little mole shook his head. "How I wish I could read. Then I wouldn't be so lonely."

"Well, we are going to change this right now," said Dusty firmly. "You're going home with me."

"Oh no, I couldn't do that. Nobody wants me around. It would be very dangerous for me to—"

Dusty put up his hand to stop the little mole. "I am the junior agent of the Molehole Mystery Club. You will be under my protection," he said firmly. "No one will harm you when you are with me.

"Now let's get your things packed," said Dusty, eager to get going.

Again the little mole shook his head. "I don't have anything since I lost the medal," he said sadly.

"What medal are you talking about?" demanded Dusty. His fur was standing on end. This, no doubt, could be a great clue about Moriah's medal.

"The one I found in the swamp," answered the albino.

"You found a medal in the swamp?" questioned Dusty carefully.

"Yes, it was so bright, and I liked it a lot. I carried it everywhere with me. But I lost it the other day."

"I think I know where your medal is. But you must go with me to see if it's yours," bribed Dusty. *If I can just get him to go with me back to the clubhouse, perhaps I can get him to live outside the swamp,* he thought.

"I don't like to go where I'm not wanted," responded the albino.

"You won't feel unwanted by my friends," assured Dusty. "They are wonderful and not prejudiced at all. They won't mind your being white."

"Are you sure?"

"I'm sure. Now let's go." Dusty opened the door to the creepy house and let the albino go in front of him. As he did so an uneasy thought came to his mind.

Are my friends really not prejudiced? he wondered. As he thought about it he remembered Morty's prejudice against girls. Then he thought of Snarkey and how he always called Otis "Pudge" and made fun of him.

Dusty knew prejudice meant you had your mind already made up that somebody was not good, even before you met him. Would his friends also be prejudiced against the white mole with no name? It wasn't a pleasant thought.

THE SUSPICION

Later that day, when Dusty introduced the albino at the Club, the members stared at the strange looking mole. *So this is the ghost,* they thought. It seemed almost funny they had been so frightened of this shy creature.

"Morty, will you get Moriah's medal, please?" asked the junior agent. "I want to see if it's the same one my friend found."

As Morty held it out to the albino, the white animal suddenly lost his shyness. "That's it!" he cried. "That's the medal I found."

"Found?" questioned Snarkey in a sarcastic voice. "Where?"

"In the swamp," said the white mole, who was under suspicion.

"No way!" said Mortimer. "This medal belonged to an old mole, Moriah. He never goes into the swamp."

Dusty looked at them warningly. He knew their harsh words and tones would frighten the shy mole. He was right, for when the white mole saw they didn't believe him, he darted past them straight out the door.

"Wait, Friend!" shouted Dusty. "They don't understand."

But it was too late. The albino mole was gone.

"Now see what you've done," said Dusty. "You've frightened him away."

"He wouldn't have run off like that if he weren't guilty," accused Snarkey.

"I don't think he's who he claims to be," said Mortimer. "Did you notice his eyes? They're *pink!*" he said with disgust. "I bet he's a *girl* in disguise."

Dusty stood looking at his friends with sorrow. "You guys make me sick! You are all prejudiced, that's what!"

The club members stared at their leader. "You had your minds made up before you even met him. His eyes are pink because he's an albino. The poor fellow doesn't

even have a name because his parents rejected him. They thought there was something wrong with him too."

Sadly Dusty told the story of the lonely little mole who had been rejected all of his life because he looked different. As he told about him, a tear found its way down Musty's face. Penelope blew her nose loudly.

"And now we've driven him off," finished the leader sadly.

"I'm really sorry, Dusty," said Snarkey. "I didn't mean to hurt him. But it did seem like he stole the medal. I didn't mean to be prejudiced."

"You know, guys, I've been thinking about this. I wonder if all of us aren't a bit prejudiced. I mean, think about it, Morty. You really are prejudiced about girls."

Mort hung his head. He knew their leader was right.

"And Snarkey, how about your prejudice toward Otis? You're always calling him Pudge. I'm sure he doesn't appreciate your calling attention to his weight problem. I think we all have certain things we're prejudiced about."

Musty spoke up. "I wasn't very nice to him either. I thought he had stolen the medal, even before I heard about it."

Dusty shook his head and continued. "That medal the albino found is the only thing the little fellow had in the world."

"I say we follow him," said Morty. "Poor guy. We're all at fault he ran away. With Sammy Shrew around he'll need all kinds of help."

"Let's go," agreed all of the mole members.

Quickly the moles made their way to Mossy Roots
Swamp. As they raced along Dusty worried about his
new friend. What if Sammy Shrew was at the mansion
when the albino returned?

Nearing the mansion, they heard loud noises and
angry voices.

"Get him!" they heard Sammy Shrew shout. "Don't
let him get away."

"He's gone upstairs," yelled another thug. "After him!"

Dusty and his friends crept silently into the house and up the stairs. As they came to the top of the steps, Dusty put out his hand and stopped them.

Standing in the hallway was the white mole facing the thugs and Sammy. In his paws he was holding jewelry and several other items.

"Looking for these?" he said calmly to the thugs.

"That's our stuff!" screamed Sammy Shrew, lunging at the mole.

"Not on your life!" said the albino bravely, taking a step backward.

Sammy and the thugs rushed at the little mole, snarling and showing their teeth. The albino moved away quickly. Suddenly the rug on which the thugs were standing gave way. A trap door yawned, and Sammy and his thugs plunged to the lower story of the mansion.

The albino looked up at the moles, who were staring at him. "I guess that takes care of those thieves," he said. "Here is the rest of their loot."

Mortimer stepped forward and took the items from the mole. "So this is how the medal got into the swamp," he said sheepishly. "And they stole all this other stuff too."

"Snarkey, go downstairs and get those characters tied up before they try anything else," commanded Dusty. Turning to the albino he said, "Please forgive us, Alby. I'm sorry we didn't believe you at first."

The white mole looked at Dusty suspiciously. "What did you say?" he asked.

"I said, please forgive us—" began Dusty.

"No, I mean, what did you call me?" inquired the albino.

"Why, I called you—Alby. I'm sorry. It just slipped out. I didn't mean to call attention to—"

The albino's pink eyes were filling with tears again. "Please don't apologize. That's the most beautiful thing I ever heard. You gave me a name! Alby! Oh, thank you, Dusty!" said the albino mole, putting out his paw.

Dusty felt a lump in his throat. It was so big he couldn't answer his new friend. "Are you ready to go home, Alby?" he asked, shaking the white mole's paw.

"I'm ready," agreed Alby.

"I think I know someone who deserves a medal," stated the junior agent as the moles started downstairs.

"Who's that?" asked his new friend.

"Why, the newest member of the Molehole Mystery Club, Alby Mole," said Dusty.

The other members of the Molehole Mystery Club stood at the bottom of the steps cheering as Dusty and the new club member came down the steps.

"This was quite a case, wasn't it, Pudg—uh, Otis?" said Snarkey as they left the Swamp Mansion.

"Yup! Quite a case," agreed Otis, squeezing through the thorn bush.

The moles weren't sorry to leave Mossy Root Swamp and the mansion behind. All of them were wondering where the next adventure of the Molehole Mystery Club would take them.

THROUGH THE SPYGLASS

Would you like to know more about Alby and how he's getting along? Take a peek through my spyglass. We see him now living happily with Dusty and Musty in their home. He is attending the Molesbury Elementary School and quickly catching up to his new friends.

Since becoming a member of the Molehole Mystery Club, Alby has made some wonderful friendships. All of the members have a new love and respect for each other now that Alby is part of the club.

Although some at school still make fun of his white fur and tease him, most have learned to love and accept him, in spite of his difference. The white mole is content and happier than he has ever been in his life.

The moles in Molesbury are learning some things that kids need to learn. They're learning that the color of your skin or the way you talk and other differences are not important. What is most important is what is inside the heart. A verse in the Bible puts it very well. It says, "Man looks at the outward appearance, but the Lord looks at the heart" (1 Samuel 16:7, *New International Version*).

We can learn from the little moles not to judge one another by how we look. By listening to each other, we can understand why we have differences.

Take one final peek through the spyglass. Alby has found something he can do to help others. He and his Molehole Mystery Club friends are now working with some little moles in Molesbury who are handicapped. They are showing love to them and helping them to know they are important in the Lord's plan for His world.

Perhaps there are some things you can do to help others less fortunate than yourself. Look around you. There is someone you can help.

UNDERGROUND
"DIG-TIONARY"

ALBINO (al-bī-nō): A human or animal that lacks enough pigment to color skin, hair, and eyes.

Have you ever seen a cute, white rabbit with pink eyes? That was an albino rabbit. The word *albino* means "colorless," or "white." An albino animal is one that is born without the color pigments that give natural color to the hair, skin, and eyes. Albinos occur in all species of life.

Most albinos find it hard to survive in the wild. Their eyes are often weaker than normal, and they are usually less physically strong and coordinated. The white coloring also makes them easy prey for other animals.

TRUE albinos have pink eyes. The reason their eyes are pink is that the tiny blood vessels of the iris (the part of the eye that has color) show through. This is because the normal color is missing.

Sometimes albinos are rejected by their parents and own kind and are driven from their natural habitats (homes). Human albinos often face ridicule because they are different. Albinism is a condition that deserves our understanding and concern—whether found in a human or in animals. God, the Creator of all, has His own purpose in allowing some of His creation to be different in this way.

JOIN
MOLEHOLE MYSTERY
CLUB

Would you like to join the Molehole Mystery Club? This will entitle you to receive your very own Molehole Mystery Club ID card and Dusty's free newsletter. The newsletter will be filled with clues and mysteries you can solve and lots of fun things to do.

The newsletter will share things with you from God's Word that will help you live a happy life as a child of God. My spyglass shows me some wonderful words from the Bible that you need to remember always.

These verses are the Molehole Mystery Club Motto, and you will need to memorize them to become a member. The words are found in the Bible [1 Thessalonians 5:21 and 22]: "Test everything. Hold on to the good. Avoid [stay away from] every kind of evil" *(New International Version)*.

We'll be looking for your membership application for our club. See you in the next Molehole adventure story. Happy reading!

MOLEHOLE MYSTERY SERIES

Dusty and Musty are at it again, solving more mysteries. And you can be a part of the fun!

Join in with Dusty and the rest of the club and experience lots of neat adventures with them in **Dusty Mole, Private Eye; Secret at Mossy Root Mansion; The Gypsies' Secret; Foul Play at Moler Park; The Upstairs Connection;** and **The Hare-Brained Habit.**

All of the books in the Molehole Mystery Series are filled with the underground mystery and intrigue of your junior agent friends Dusty and

Musty Mole and the rest of the Mystery Club: Morty, Millard, Alby, Penney, Snarkey, Alfred, and Otis.

Don't let the villianous Sammy Shrew catch you by surprise. You can be on the inside track by joining the Molehole Mystery Club.

If you would like to be a member of the Molehole Mystery Club and hear more about the adventures of Dusty and Musty, fill out the card below and send it in. By being an official member, you will receive six issues of the newsletter, *The Underground Gazette,* and your own I.D. card.

MOLEHOLE MYSTERY CLUB MEMBERSHIP APPLICATION

DATE:_____

NAME: _____

ADDRESS: _____

CITY, STATE: _____ ZIP:_____

AGE: _____ BIRTHDATE: _____

___ CHECK HERE IF YOU HAVE MEMORIZED
    OUR MOTTO VERSES,

1 THESSALONIANS 5:21 - 22.
"Test everything. Hold on to the good. Stay away from every kind of evil."

Wait a minute, you mean the card is missing! Well you can still be a member of the Molehole Mystery Club by just sending in your name and address to:

Molehole Mystery Club
Lock Box 10064
Chicago, IL 60610-0064

Place
Stamp
Here

Molehole Mystery Club
Lock Box 10064
Chicago, IL 60610-0064